This Walker book belongs to:

....

....

....

To the Utterly Lovely Kellys

Niall, Niamh, Mary, Steve and Ann

First published 2011 by Walker Books Ltd
87 Vauxhall Walk, London SE11 5HJ

This edition published 2012

2 4 6 8 10 9 7 5 3 1

Printed in China

British Library Cataloguing in Publication Data:
a catalogue record for this book is available
from the British Library

ISBN 978-1-4063-3774-7

www.walker.co.uk

WALKER BOOKS
AND SUBSIDIARIES

LONDON • BOSTON • SYDNEY • AUCKLAND

Utterly Lovely One

Mary Murphy

Oh, my Yummy One,
my Utterly Lovely One!
Look at you,
so gorgeous.

You know,
my Yummy One,
the world is full of
utterly lovely ones.
Yes it is!

Like this
frilled lizard,
fancy and
fabulous,
perky even
in the
midday sun.

And,
my Yummy One,
just look at
Baby Elephant!
That wonderful
nose ...

those kind,
gentle eyes ...

and the way
her ears sit
on her utterly
lovely head.

Here comes
Dragonfly,
darting on his
flashing wings,

and Snail,
slow and careful.

Both little.
Both quiet.
Both utterly lovely.

And Jungle Bird,
with his loud
laughing voice...

The things he says!
The songs he sings!

I can tell, Yummy One,
that you want
to sing with him.

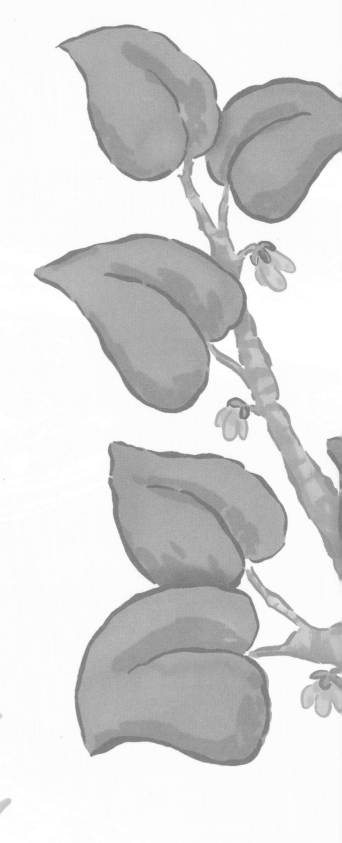

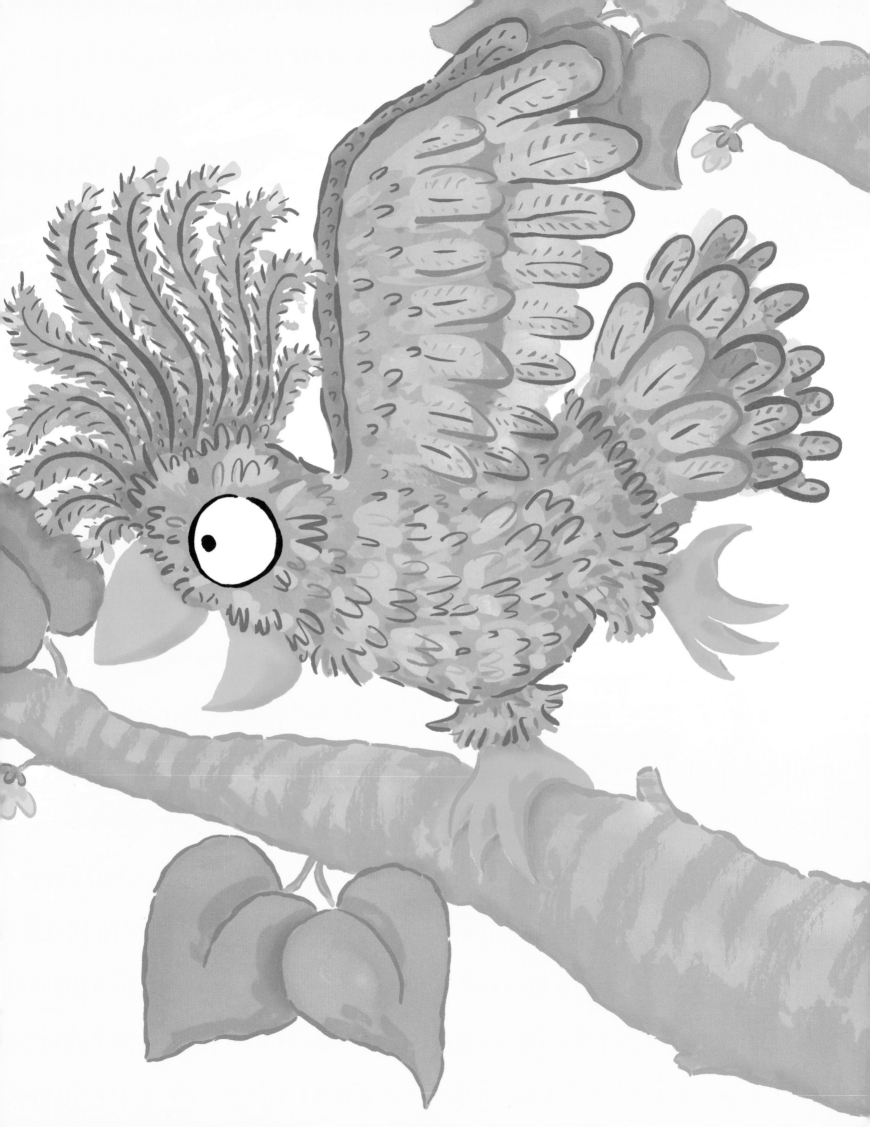

Numbat is so nice
that wherever she goes
everyone feels nice,
just because
Numbat is there.

Even Armadillo, usually so shy...
Suddenly he is brave enough
to make friends.
Suddenly he feels nice.
And he is more than nice —
he is utterly lovely.

Look, here's Crocodile —
always ready for action,
with a grin that takes
up his whole head.

He knows he is handsome!
He knows he is smart!

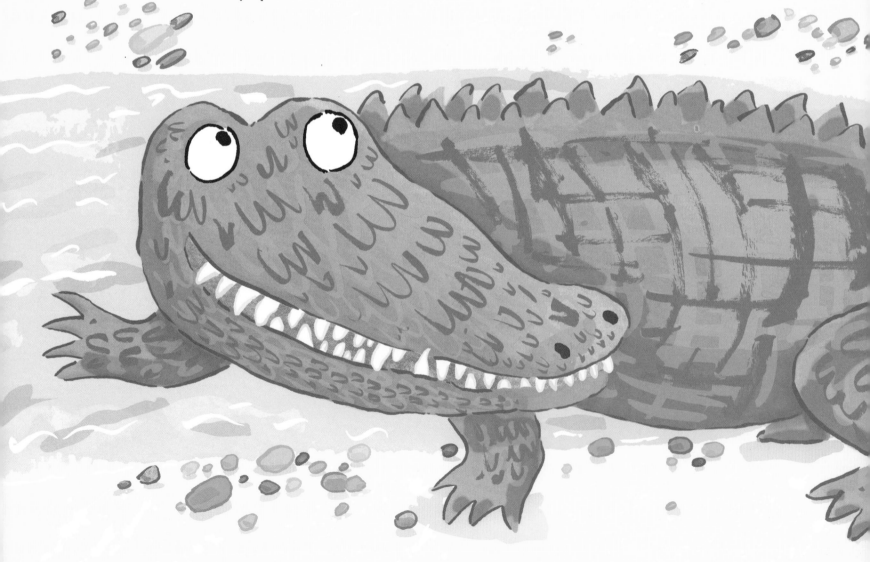

He knows he is
utterly lovely.

And the monkeys, well...
They're so funny!
They're so tricky!
They just want to play and play.

Couldn't you
watch them
all day?

Soft little Bushbaby,
with her huge shining eyes,
holding on tight
with every finger and toe.

She is lovely,
utterly.

Yes, the world
is full of
utterly lovely ones.
Amazing! Dazzling!
Astonishing!
Each one
a delight.

And how great!
How marvellous!
How lucky for me ...
that of all those
lovely ones,
you are
my one,

my Utterly

Lovely One.

Other books by Mary Murphy:

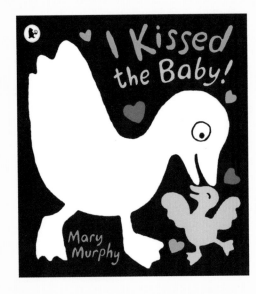

ISBN 978-1-4063-2996-4

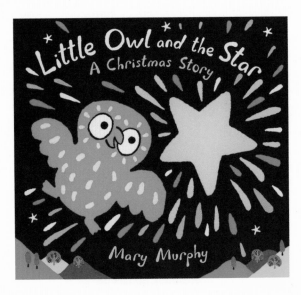

ISBN 978-1-4063-0186-1

Available from all good booksellers

www.walker.co.uk